Contents

A first book of

Aesop's Fables

retold by Marie Stuart

with illustrations by
Robert Ayton

Publishers: Ladybird Books Ltd . Loughborough
© Ladybird Books Ltd 1974
Printed in England

The fox without a tail

One day a fox ran into a trap.
He pulled and pulled to get away
from it.
At last he did, but his tail came off.
It was left in the trap.

He did not like the way he looked
without a tail.
"All the other foxes will make fun
of me," he said.

"What can I do?"
I know, I will make them think
it is better not to have a tail."

5

So he said to the other foxes,
"You would look better without
tails. What use are they anyway?
Look at me. I can run very fast
because I have no tail."

But one old fox said,
"You say that, only because you
have lost your own tail.
That is why you do not want us
to have tails. But we like our tails.
And we shall keep them,
thank you."

Moral :
Wise people are not easily fooled.

The shepherd boy and the wolf

Once there was a boy who lived
on a farm. Every day he had to take
his father's sheep to a hill a long
way off. He did not like being there
on his own.

One day, he said to himself,
"I will call Wolf! Wolf!
Then everyone will think that
a wolf has come to eat my sheep.

People will run to help me.
It will be fun when they find out
there is no wolf after all."

So he did call "Wolf! Wolf!"
and everyone ran
to help him.

8

When they came he did not thank them. He just said, "There is no wolf. It was only a joke. Now you will all have to go back home again."

He did this three times. Each time he told them that there was no wolf.

Then one day the wolf **did** come.
"Help! help! The wolf is here!"
called the boy.

But everyone said,
"We know that there is no wolf.
He just calls us for fun.
There is no danger.
This time we will not go."

So they did not go
and the wolf killed all the sheep.

Moral:

If we tell lies, no one will believe us
when we speak the truth.

The boastful traveller

A man once went to a place
he had never been to before. It was
a long way off and he was there
for a year. When he went home,
he wanted to talk about
it all the time.

Everyone said,
"Why is he always telling us about
that place? We don't want to know
about it."

They asked him, "Why did you come
back if it was so nice?"

"I came back to tell you about it,"
said the man,
and he went on talking.

"In that place," he said,
"all the men can jump well.
One day we wanted to see who
could jump the best. So we all
had a try. My jump was the best.
I am a very good jumper.
If you had been there at the time,
you would have seen
how good I am."

"We do not have to go all that way
to see you jump," said one of
the men. "You can let us see how
well you can do it here.
So jump **now!**"

Moral:
*People who boast are soon found
out.*

The crow and the fox

One day a big, black crow, found
some cheese.
"I will fly up into this tree with it,"
she said.
"I want to eat it now."

A fox came by and saw the bird.
He saw the cheese as well.
He, too, wanted to eat the cheese.

He went round and round the tree
while he thought how he could
get the cheese.

Then he said to the crow,
"You look very nice. If you can sing
very nicely as well, I think you
must be Queen of all the birds."

The crow was very pleased.
She liked to be called a Queen.
"Yes, I can sing," she said.

But as she said this
the cheese fell from her beak.

18

Down to the ground it fell. The fox picked up the cheese and ran away.

"You may be Queen of the birds. You may look nice and you may sing well. But you do not think very well," he said, as he ran off.

Moral:

Beware of people who say nice things they do not mean.

Who will bell the cat

Once some mice lived in a house.

A big cat lived in the house too.

Every day she liked to eat
some of the mice.

At last they said to one another,
"This must stop, or soon we shall
all be eaten. Let us all think
what we can do."

After a time an old mouse said,
"I know what we can do. One
of us must put a bell on the cat.

The bell will tell us when she is
near and when we must stay
at home.
After she has gone away, we can
come out again."

"Yes. That will be a wise thing to do.
Let us do that," they all said.

"But which one of us will put the bell on her?" said the old mouse.

"I am too old, I cannot run very fast so I don't think I can do it."

"So are we,"
said some of the others.

"And we are too little,"
said the baby mice.

In the end no-one would do it.
So the bell was never put on the cat and she went on eating the mice.

Moral:
Some things are more easily said than done.

The crow and the swan

A crow once saw a swan
and said to her, "How nice you look!
I wish I were white like you.
I do not like being black."

He saw that the swan was always
in the water.

"If I get in the water,
I may become white too," he said.

So he got into the water, but he
was still black when he came out.

"Let me think," he said.
"If I **stay** in the water
that may make me white."

25

Before the crow went into the water, he could fly about to look for food. He always found something to eat.

He did not like fish and could find nothing else to eat in the water.

So he did not live very long, nor did he become white.

Moral:

Think well before you copy other people.

The wolf and the lamb

A big, bad wolf saw a little white lamb and wanted to eat her.

He did not eat her at once.
He tried to think of a good excuse for killing her.

Then people would not think he was a bad wolf.

So he said to the lamb,
"Last year you called me
very bad names."

"But I am only a baby. I was not
born last year," said the lamb.

"Well then, you ate my dinner,"
the wolf said next.

"But I could not eat your dinner,"
said the lamb.
"I am too little, I can only drink."

"That's it! You drank my water,"
said the wolf.

"But I can only drink my mother's
milk,"
said the lamb.

"Is that so?"
said the wolf.

"But **I** can eat and
I am going to eat
you.

I am going to do it now
because I want my dinner at once!"

With that, he jumped on the little
lamb. And that was the end of her.

Moral:

*People who want to do something
bad can always find an excuse.*

The lion and the hare

Once a lion found a hare.
He was just going to eat her
when a stag ran by.

"That stag will make me a bigger
dinner," he said.

So he let the hare go and ran after
the stag. But the stag could run
very, very fast and soon it got
right away.

When the lion saw that he could
not catch the stag,
he said, "I will go back for the hare."

But when he came to the place
where the hare had been,
he found that she had gone.

"I should have had her for my

dinner when I first saw her,"
said the lion. "I wanted too much
and now I have nothing."

Moral:
*It is sometimes wiser to be content
with what you have.*

Brother and sister

Once there was a man who had
two children, a boy and a girl.
The boy was good looking,
but the girl was not.

One day they found a mirror and
for the first time, saw what they
looked like. The boy was very
pleased. He said to his sister,
"How handsome I am!
I look much nicer than you!"

The girl did not like what he said
and gave her brother a push.
"Go away!" she said.

Their father saw what was
happening and said to the boy,
"You must always **be** good as well
as **look** good."

And to the girl he said,

"My dear, if you help everyone and do your best to please, everyone will love you. It will not matter that you are not as good looking as your brother."

Moral:

*It is better to **be** good than to be just good looking.*

The goose that laid
the golden eggs

Once an old man and an old
woman had a goose. Their goose
was not like other geese
because its eggs were different.
They were made of gold.

Every day
the goose laid a golden egg
for the old man and the old woman.

They sold the eggs for a lot of
money. But the more money they
had the more they wanted.

They said,
"If our goose lays golden eggs
she must be made of gold.
So let us cut her open
and get out all the gold at once.
Then we will have more money."

So they killed the goose, but found
no gold.

When their goose was cut open
they saw that
she was just like any other goose.

42

And after that there were no more golden eggs. So they did not get any more money. They had nothing left in the end.

Moral:
A greedy man can lose all he has.

The wind and the sun

One day the wind said to the sun, "Look at that man walking along the road. I can get his cloak off more quickly than you can."

"We will see about that," said the sun. "I will let you try first."

So the wind tried to make the man take off his cloak. He blew and blew, but the man only pulled his cloak more closely around himself.

"I give up,"
said the wind at last.
"I cannot get his cloak off."
Then the sun tried.
He shone as hard as he could.
The man soon became hot
and took off his cloak.

"I have won," said the sun.
"I made him take his cloak off."

Moral:
Kindness often gets things done more quickly than force.

The trees and the axe

Once a man wanted to cut down
some trees to make a house,
but he could not use his axe
because it had no handle.

So he went to the top of a hill
where there were many trees
and said to them,
"May I take a tree from this hill?"

But he did not tell them why.

The trees said to one another,
"Let us give him a very little tree.
Then he will go away
and not ask us for anything more."

So they gave him a little tree
and the man went home.
When he got there
he made a handle for his axe.

Then he went back to the hill and began to cut down the other trees.

"If we had not let him have the little tree he could not have cut us down," they said.

But it was too late to stop him.

Moral:

Be careful when you give way over small things, or you may have to give way over big ones.

AESOP was probably a slave who lived in Greece about 2,500 years ago. He was ugly and deformed but very clever. His fables made him famous.

After a while he was set free by his master and then lived at the court of King Croesus. It is said that his life ended when he went to the Temple of Apollo at Delphi. He made the Delphians angry and they pushed him over a cliff.